Printed and Published in Great Britain by D. C. Thomson & Co., Ltd.,
185 Fleet Street, London EC4A 2HS.
© D. C. THOMSON & CO., LTD., 1998   ISBN 0-85116-674-1
(Certain stories do not appear exactly as originally published.)

AROUND THE WORLD IN 60 YEARS

with THE BEANO and THE DANDY

The Bash Street Kids are in a tropical paradise on the first stage of their World Tour (from The Beano of 1967) and throughout this book we'll be following their hilarious journey. Each country they visit has a special significance for some of The Beano and The Dandy folk from the past and present that you'll meet, so let's set off right away on our sixty-year journey through comic land!

Somewhere across the ocean fr[om] the Bash Street Kids' first stop is [a] small, unnamed island, where a nearby shipwreck has a tale to te[ll] from The Beano of the '50s, of fiv[e] brave survivors:-

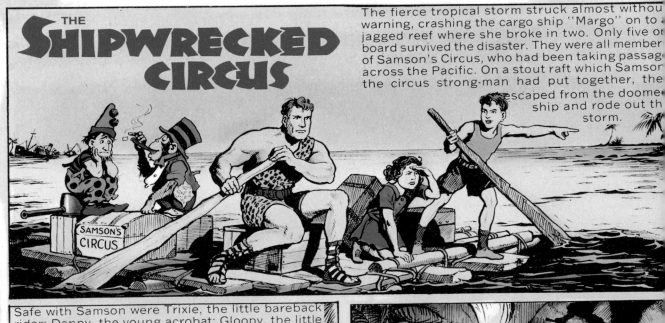

THE SHIPWRECKED CIRCUS

The fierce tropical storm struck almost withou[t] warning, crashing the cargo ship "Margo" on to [a] jagged reef where she broke in two. Only five o[n] board survived the disaster. They were all member[s] of Samson's Circus, who had been taking passag[e] across the Pacific. On a stout raft which Samson the circus strong-man had put together, the[y] escaped from the doome[d] ship and rode out th[e] storm.

SAMSON'S CIRCUS

Safe with Samson were Trixie, the little bareback rider; Danny, the young acrobat; Gloopy, the little clown; and Horace, the educated ape. They were all thankful to reach the safety of a nearby island.

SUGAR

D.D.W.

That night the ca[st]aways sheltered in [a] cave and soon began [to] recover from their orde[al]

At the first opportunity Samson, Danny and Gloopy returned to the ''Margo'' to salvage what they could from the wreck.

Carefully they approached the broken ship on the deadly reef.

Slowly the raft drifted inside one of the gaping holds.

Danny and Gloopy began to help Samson load the raft with circus gear which lay in the hold.

A great octopus was lurking in the inky-black water. It seized Samson in its powerful tentacles and pulled him off the raft.

Beside Danny lay a box of weapons which had been used in one of the circus acts. Swiftly, the boy thrust a sword into Samson's hand before it disappeared from sight.

The sword saved Samson's life. With all his might he drove it into the octopus, killing it instantly.

Danny and Gloopy yelled with joy as the strong man climbed safely back aboard the raft.

MY HOME TOWN *Nassau*

NASSAU is a tourist centre and holiday resort on New Providence, a small island in the Bahamas. In the past, Nassau wasn't quite such a happy place—it was a centre of piracy, gun-running and rum-smuggling.

Every Boxing Day and New Year's Day, the inhabitants of Nassau celebrate with a festival called "Junkanoo". The people, wearing fancy dress and ringing cowbells, form a procession behind colourfully-decorated floats.

For eight years, between 1962 and 1970, a prize-page in "The Dandy" asked readers to write about their home towns, little knowing just how far away some Dandy readers lived! How's this for an exotic beginning — The Bahamas! You'll find other far-away "Home Towns" throughout the book.

To protect the island from Napoleon's navy, forts were built on the east and west coasts. Here we see the cannon of Fort Charlotte, which stands on the eastern side of the island.

A favourite sport amongst holiday visitors to Nassau is sea-angling. The waters just off the shore are teeming with fish of all sizes and many kinds, and for anyone who wants to catch something really big, tackle capable of landing a fish weighing well over quarter of a ton can be hired.

During the American Civil War (1861-1865), Nassau was one of the ports used by ships smuggling guns to the Southern States.

WAHOOOOOOOOOO!

This is one fish that the first-time angler should keep well away from. Its streamlined shape and muscular body make it a hot handful even for an expert. It does have an interesting name, though. It's called a "Wahoo"!

Parts of the film, "Thunderball", starring Sean Connery in the role of James Bond, were shot in and around Nassau.

Does any famous person live in your town?
Do they make glass eyes in your town?
Is any kind of funny festival held in your town?

Write about your home town and win a DANDY prize. Anything interesting or out of the ordinary —that's what to write about. And just two or three items are enough.

On the east side of New Providence stands the ru of a tower which is supposed to have been the hom of Edward Teach, better known as Blackbeard, on of the most wicked pirates who ever sailed the se Blackbeard died in 1718, in a battle with th English lieutenant, Maynard.

Remember to put your name, age and address on your entry and say which prize you would like best from this list.

COMPLETE COWBOY OUTFIT, NURSE'S OUTFIT, BALL BEARING ROLLER SKATES, £1 POSTAL ORDER.

SEND YOUR ENTRY TO-
"MY HOME TOWN"
"The Dandy"
18a Hollingsworth St.,
London N. 7.

Next port of call for the Bash Street Kids' world cruise is the U.S.A. — home of tall buildings, huge ranches, and big men like Desperate Dan. The flag is nicknamed "The Stars and Stripes" and you'll see some of the stars from The Dandy and The Beano on the following pages.

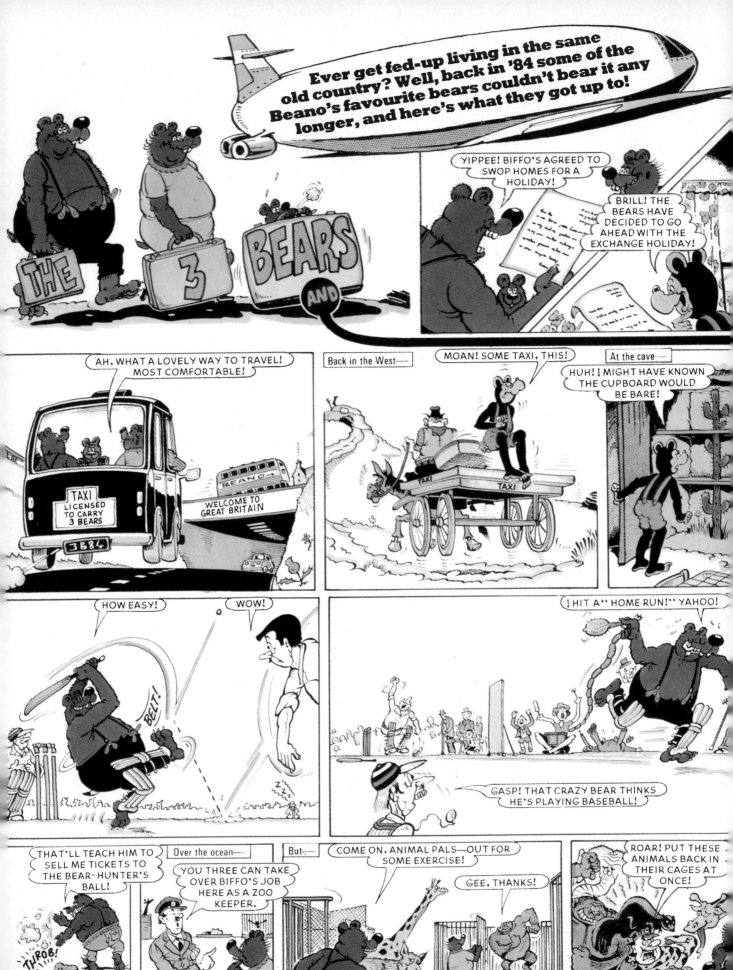

1984

BIFFO THE BEAR

DESPERATE DAN

A DAN'S WORLD

In a series of episodes in the mid '50s, Desperate Dan had been mistakenly chased by the police and had opted for disguising himself in an attempt to hide. Do you think you would recognise him . . . ?

1955

Jammy Mr Sammy

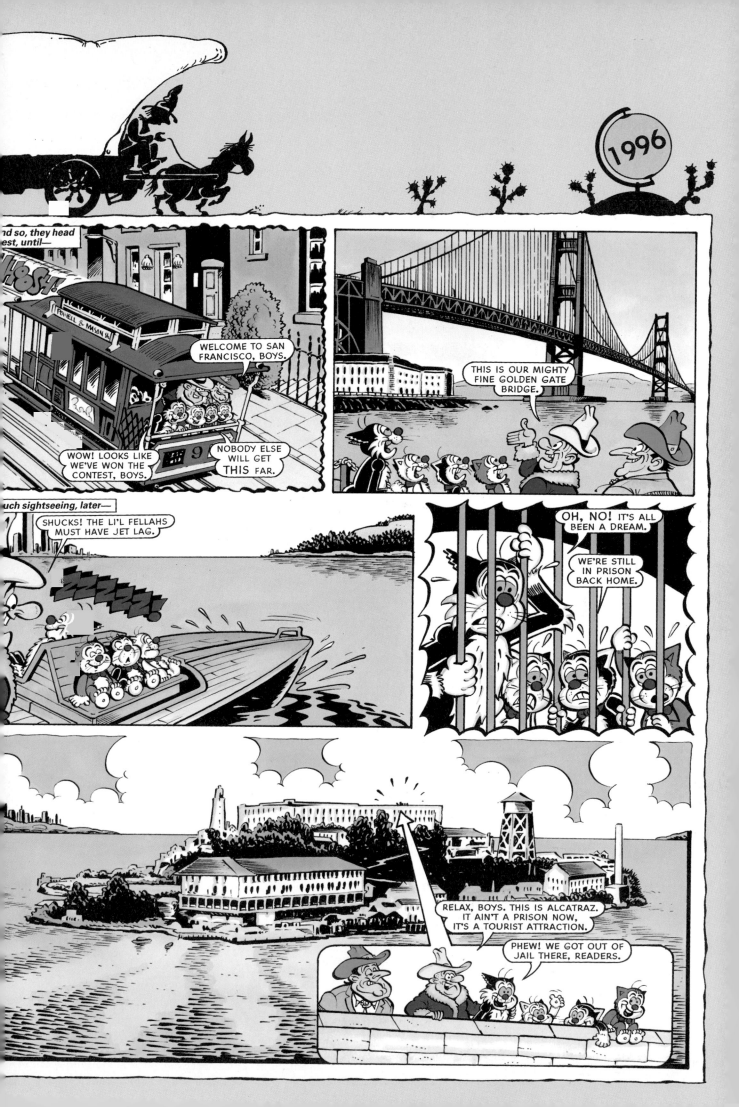

MONTREAL is the largest city in Canada. It is on Montreal Island, in the St Lawrence River, in the province of Quebec. Although it is about 1000 miles from the Atlantic, Montreal is an important seaport, and large ocean-going cargo ships can reach it.

Although Montreal is of such importance as a port, it is only open for seven months of the year. From mid-November to April each year, the St Lawrence River is frozen over and no ships can reach the city.

Montreal Island was discovered by Jacques Cartier, the famous French explorer, in 1535. He was welcomed to the island by a large band of Huron Indians who took him to their stockaded settlement. There, he held prayers with them and read to them from the Gospel of St John. The stamp above shows Cartier on the left, and another famous French explorer, Samuel Champlain, on the right.

Until its conquest by the British in 1760, Montreal belonged to France. Today, although Canada is part of the British Commonwealth, most of Montreal's population are of French descent, and French is spoken more than English.

Montreal's biggest attraction at present is Expo 67, the huge World's Fair. The Fair, which lasts until October 27, marks Canada's centenary. Expo 67 is situated on two islands in the St Lawrence River, islands which were largely man-made especially for the Fair. It cost 350 million pounds to prepare and about 70 nations are taking part. For the millions of visitors who visit the Exhibition, there is every kind of entertainment it is possible to imagine.

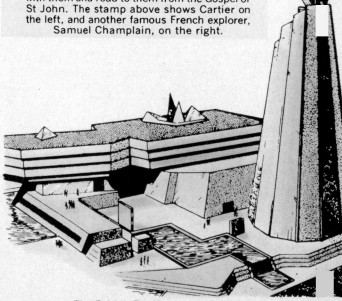

The British Pavilion was designed by the famous architect, Sir Basil Spence. Its most striking feature is the 200-foot-high tower with the three-dimensional Union Jack on top. Inside you are shown around by charming mini-skirted British hostesses.

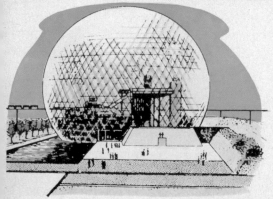

America's pavilion at Expo 67 is a huge, twenty-storey, transparent "bubble" which glistens in the sunlight. The overhead minirail, which carries visitors all round the exhibition, actually passes through the middle of this pavilion.

This is the Canadian Pavilion, known as the Katimavik, which is an Eskimo word for a meeting-place. It is the biggest pavilion, and inside you can see many aspects of Canadian life and history.

When the Dandy Wonder-dog Black Bob's master, Andrew Glen, went to Canada to help a friend, Bob found that not everyone was friendly!

1964

1941

GOOGLY THE ESKIMO

1. See me
Get fish for tea.
It's eas-ee.

2. With skis
I get teas
With ease.

3. What's there?
I declare
It's a bear.

4. Oh, boy,
Let's employ
A decoy.

5. He's here.
Take out spear.
He'll disappear.

6. He's gone. Where?
We don't care.
Goodbye, bear!

Ten years ago The Beano's Dennis the Menace went farther than most people on a sledge — he went all the way to the Arctic!

DENNIS the MENACE

and **GNASHER**

1988

IN- "THE GREAT SLEDGE RACE"

EITHER GNASHER'S AGED SUDDENLY, OR IT'S SNOWING!

HAW-HAW!

YAHOO! SNOW AT LAST! MUST GET MY SLEDGE OUT!

TUG

TOY CUPBOARD

TOPPLE

FLOP!

THE SNOW WILL BE FOLLOWED BY A SUDDEN THAW

ZOOM!

I WARNED YOU!

SUDDEN THAW

SUDDEN THAW

ERK!

CLUNK!

WINNING POST

WE'RE GOING TO DO IT!

LITTLE DID YOU KNOW MY DOGS ARE HIGHLY TRAINED PERFORMING POODLES!

WE'RE GOING TO LOSE, UNLESS...

I'LL DO A DEAL...

ZOOM!

TA!

MIGHTY PUSH

WINNING POST

JUDGE

THE WINNER!

ZE BAH!

YAHOO!

ZOOM!

HOW DID YOU GET THAT BEAR TO HELP YOU?

← READER

PEOPLE WILL DO ANYTHING FOR A DENNIS AND GNASHER T-SHIRT!

GROWL HEH!

Dennis

The U.K.

STAMPEDING quickly over the U.K. on their journey around the globe, the Bash Street Kids (who first stampeded through the pages of the Beano back in 1954) haven't time to meet anyone, but turn the page and you'll meet Winker Watson, Just Jimmy, Bully Beef and Chips, Minnie the Minx and other classic characters in this truly British section.

WINKER WATSON

WINKER WATSON was a wizard. Not the kind of wizard who casts magic spells, although sometimes his tricks left the Masters at Greytowers School spellbound.

No, Winker was a wizard at wangling. If ever any of Winker's mates in the Third Form wanted to skip prep, or to sneak off to the cinema, or to dodge some punishment, it was Winker to whom they turned. He could wangle it! In fact, he was the champion wangler of all time.

Today was one of those days when some super wangling was going to be necessary. Winker knew it when he heard Mr Creep, the nasty Third Form Master, spring an unpleasant surprise.

- COLLECT IN THE EXERCISE BOOKS, WATSON. I'M GIVING THE CLASS A TEST—AND I DON'T WANT ANY FUNNY BUSINESS GOING ON.
- YESSIR, MR CREEP, SIR! HAND IT OVER, TROTTY—YOU'RE NOT TO BE TRUSTED!
- OOH! LOOK WHO'S TALKING!

- PUT THEM ON MY DESK FOR NOW, WATSON!
- YES, SIR!

Winker obeyed to the letter. He placed the books very carefully indeed, in just the right spot to start off a wangle.

When Creepy returned to his desk, he began searching around on it, and a worried look spread over his face.

- THAT'S FUNNY—I CAN'T FIND MY FOUNTAIN PEN! OH, DEAR, I HOPE IT'S NOT LOST. IT'S THE GOLD ONE AUNT AGATHA GAVE ME FOR MY BIRTHDAY...!

- COME HERE, WATSON! DID YOU TAKE MY GOLD PEN FROM MY DESK?
- ME, MR CREEP, SIR? I OF COURSE NOT, SIR. SEARCH ME IF YOU LIKE!

Creepy was so suspicious, he did just that. He made Winker turn out his pockets.

No pen there! So Creepy set about turning the whole classroom upside down. Talk about hunt the thimble!

- OH, DEAR, DO HURRY UP AND FIND IT, BOYS, OR WE WON'T HAVE TIME FOR THE TEST BEFORE THE BELL GOES!
- HEE-HEE! THAT'S WHAT WE'RE HOPING!

Boodle was so terribly angry that he plunged his hand straight back into the hat without thinking.

- GURR! I BET SOMEBODY HAS BEEN TAMPERING WITH THIS! I'LL TRY AGAIN...
- BETTER LUCK THIS TIME, MASTER ROBIN!

But Boodle's luck was no better. In fact, it was worse!

- YEOWL!
- THAT MAKES A CHANGE, MASTER ROBIN—A MOUSETRAP!
- SNAP!

Boodle's troubles weren't over yet. As he was being doctored by Jenks, an angry voice could be heard from outside.

- LET ME PUT A BANDAGE ON YOUR FINGER, MASTER ROBIN—ER, SORRY I LAUGHED. I THOUGHT THAT WAS MEANT TO HAPPEN!
- HEY! WHOSE WHITE RABBITS ARE THESE IN MY GARDEN?
- OH, DEAR! I BET THEY'RE MINE!

The bellows of rage were coming from Jarvis, the janitor. The rabbits which should have been in Boodle's hat were eating the janitor's lettuce!

- HURRY UP AND CATCH THEM, OR I'LL REPORT YOU TO THE HEADMASTER!
- OO-ER! COME HERE, SNOWY!

With Boodle out of the way, Winker and his pal Tim Trott had a great chance to raid the millionaire's room.

- COME ON, TROTTY, LET'S SEE WHAT TUCK BOODLE'S GOT HIDDEN AWAY.

It seemed that Boodle must have been pretty hungry, however, for no food was in sight.

- NONE ON THE TABLE, WINKER. HE MUST HAVE GOT IT ALL WELL HIDDEN.
- WE'LL FIND IT, TROTTY! I'LL LOOK UNDER THE BED AND YOU LOOK IN THAT CUPBOARD.

- HOORAY! I'VE FOUND SOME! HEY, WHERE ARE YOU?

Winker turned to show off the pies and cream cakes he had discovered—but Trotty had vanished!

- INSIDE THE CUPBOARD, WINKER!

Where the dickens was he? He was still absent—but his voice wasn't!

- DON'T FOOL ABOUT, TROTTY—THE CUPBOARD IS BARE!
- OTHER S... WINKER...

The secret was revealed. The cupboard was really two cupboards. Put a man in one, turn it round, open it up, and Hey Presto! No man!

- IT'S A SPECIALLY-MADE MAGICIAN'S CABINET, WINKER.
- WELL, I'M BLOWED!

Winker couldn't hope to win a contest against someone using posh equipment like this. So he set out to do what he was best at—wangling.

- YOU KEEP GUARD OUTSIDE BOODLE'S DOOR AND I'LL GET THE JANITOR'S TOOL BOX AND MAKE ONE OR TWO ALTERATIONS TO BOODLE'S TRICK CUPBOARD!
- HURRY THEN, WINKER!

Boodle had certainly spared no expense in his bid to be a better magician than Winker.

A few hours before the contest was due to start, Boodle set out all his fancy gear on the stage of the school hall. He was being his usual boastful self, too.

- YOU DON'T STAND A CHANCE, WATSON—JUST LOOK AT ALL THE MAGIC EQUIPMENT I'VE GOT!
- POOH! SO WHAT BOODLE? I'M SO JOLLY GOOD, I DON'T NEED ANY OF THAT JUNK! SEE YOU LATER!

Boodle practised all his tricks, but when he left to don his best blazer, Winker did a spot of rearranging.

- THERE'S NOBODY ABOUT, SO NOW'S MY CHANCE TO MOVE HIS DISAPPEARING CABINET TO THE SPOT ON THE STAGE WHERE I WANT IT TO BE!

1957

Although he didn't appear in The Dandy for too long (just 1956 to 1958) Just Jimmy was just right for laughs.

JUST JIMMY—
WITH A JACK-IN-THE-BOX THE FUN IS GREAT, BUT THERE'S FUNNIER FUN WITH JIM-IN-THE-CRATE!

She'd only been in The Beano for a year when this story was printed, but Minnie showed she was a maxi-Minx from her beret down to her socks!

Minnie the Minx

MINNIE! PULL YOUR SOCKS UP!

1954

OK, OK

LATER — HELPING WITH THE MESSAGES.

MINNIE! PULL YOUR SOCKS UP!

TARTS

RAGE

SPLUP

TARTS

OK, DAD! YOU HOLD THE SHOPPIN'!

DONK

MY HERO

PAH! WOULDN'T SURPRISE ME IF I HAD NIGHTMARES ABOUT SOCKS!

BEDTIME!

I DIDN'T KNOW THE WINDOW WAS OPEN AN' I THREW MY SOCKS OUTSIDE — I'LL BORROW THIS OL' NAIL FROM THE WALL AND BEND IT INTO A HOOK

CRASH!

RUSTY
1961

BULLY BEEF and CHIPS

In this classic story from The Dandy, see the beefy bull who scored
a bull's-eye with Bully Beef!

THE Bash Street Kids

1960

This story, from the early days of The Beano's Bash Street Kids, gives an all-new meaning to "long division"!

WE'RE GOING TO DIVIDE THE SCHOOL INTO FOUR 'HOUSES'. YOU ORGANISE EVERYTHING!

WE'RE GOING TO DIVIDE THE SCHOOL INTO FOUR 'HOUSES'. YOU ORGANISE EVERYTHING!

SO THE KIDS TOSS TO DECIDE ON 'HOUSE' CAPTAINS.

HEADS

HEADS!

TAILS

I'VE WON THE TOSS, HEH! HEH! NOW TO PICK THE TOUGHEST KIDS FOR MY 'HOUSE'!

RIGHT, THESE GENTLE CREATURES ARE IN MY 'HOUSE' ~ YOU WEEDS CAN SORT YOURSELVES OUT INTO THREE OTHER 'HOUSES'!

THAT'S THAT! I'LL GO AND REPORT TO THE HEADMASTER!

THE FIRST INTER-'HOUSE' COMPETITION IS "FIGHTING"! WE'LL SHOW YOU WHO'S TOP HOUSE!

RUN FOR IT, HORACE!

SQUEAK   SQUEAK   SQUEAK

THEY'VE TAKEN TO THE SEWERS! WAIT TILL I STUDY THE LIE OF THE LAND!

WHAT DANNY SEES.

BRING A CANDLE, SOMEONE!

HEE! HEE! A CRAFTY ESCAPE!

TIPTOE

WE'LL SOON DRIVE THEM OUT!

IN THE SEWER.

WHAT'S THAT FUNNY SMELL?

MAYBE IT'S GAS! -GAS?

TOO BAD THE LEAKY GAS MAIN RAN UNDER THE SCHOOL.

BOOM

QUICK! WE'LL HAVE TO TRY AND REPAIR THE DAMAGE! GET SOME BRICKS!

SO SMIFFY SETS OFF ON AN ILL-FATED MISSION.

I'LL JUST BORROW A FEW OF THESE BRICKS!

SWAY

CRASH

RUMBLE

CRACK

OMINOUS CREAK

SOUNDS LIKE THUNDER ABOUT!

MEANWHILE ~

I'VE DONE AS YOU SUGGESTED, HEADMASTER. THE SCHOOL IS NOW DIVIDED INTO ~

-AAGH! FOUR HOUSES!

I'LL SAY IT IS!

GNASHING OF TEETH

MY HOME TOWN
SHREWSBURY

1963

Footballer Arthur Rowley, player-manager of Third Division Shrewsbury Town, is Britain's top league goal-scorer. In September 1962 he scored his 411th league goal, beating the 410 goals scored by Jimmy McGrory, of Glasgow Celtic.

THIS WEEK'S WINNER—
MARION DODD (age 10), 9 CONISTON ROAD, HARLESCOTT, SHREWSBURY, wins a £1 Postal Order.

...rewsbury has one of the biggest flower shows ...Britain. It is helped by the excellent super-...sion of Percy Thrower, the "Gardening Club" ...xpert whose programme on television is so well ...nown. Percy Thrower is head of the Parks Department in Shrewsbury.

Many features of mediæval architecture still remain in Shrewsbury today. For example, in the narrow street of Grope Lane, the houses overhang the street to such an extent that from the upper windows the occupants could shake hands with their opposite neighbours.

Rowley's House Roman Museum is a doubly interesting building. Besides being a splendid example of a timber built house, it also contains an excellent collection of antiquities excavated from the remains of the old Roman town of Uriconium, which was situated just outside Shrewsbury.

In Shrewsbury stands a statue to Lord Hill. It is 132 feet high and is the tallest Doric pillar in the world. Lord Hill was one of Wellington's ablest commanders, serving in the Peninsular War and leading the famous charge against Napoleon's Imperial Guard at the Battle of Waterloo.

LORD CLIVE

In 1739 a young man tried to glide down a rope fixed from the top of the spire of St Mary's to the opposite side of the River Severn. But the rope ...apped and he fell to his death while his wife ...ecting coppers from the crowd below.

Admiral Benbow, a famous 17th Century naval commander, was born in Shrewsbury. Today his birthplace is a garage. Speaking of garages, it is claimed that the first petrol pumps ever to feed petrol straight into the tanks of cars were erected at a Shrewsbury garage.

SIR FRANCIS DRAKE ... is a story that, one of ... bowls on the Hoe, a smoo... During the game, a great ... sighted out to sea, but Sir ... the English fleet against ... finished his game of bowls! ... outnumbered, the English ... defeat the Spanis...

...well as being a great Admiral. S... ...ake was a notable Mayor of Plymo... ...was in office, he did as much as he... ...ove conditions in the town. He ha... ...carry fresh water from Dartmo... ...ymouth, and so gave the town... good water supply.

A DANDY P...

SWEYN, a Scandinavian pir... ...been the founder of Sw... Norman Conquest, and the n... ...to be derived from this ol... According to this story, Swa... "Sweyn's ey", the "ey" bein... of the River Tawe, where a Sc... was establis...

MY HOME TOWN
AYR

...PRIZE FOR EVERY READER WHOSE ...RY IS FEATURED ON THIS PAGE.

THIS WEEK'S WINNER—
EVELYN BLAKELEY (age 12), 22 QUEEN'S TERRACE, AYR, wins £1 Postal Order.

...obert Burns, Scotland's national poet, was born at ...loway, near Ayr. His early days were spent working ...a farm. But by the time he was 26. Burns became ...couraged by the hard struggle to gain a living from ...and and he decided to emigrate to Jamaica. To get ...ey for this venture, he published a volume of ...es he had been writing since boyhood. These met ...instant success and the fame of the Ayrshire ...ghman grew so great that Burns gave up his plans ...igrate. Soon after, he became an excise officer. ...s health gave out and he died at the age of 37. ...ottage where he was born was built by his father ...wadays it is visited by thousands of people from many countries every year.

Not far from Ayr is the mysterious "Electric Brae". Surprised motorists find that they are free-wheeling UP THE HILL. Similarly, cyclists find they have to pedal downhill in order to avoid running back uphill. This is caused by an optical illusion. Because of the layout of surrounding hilly scenery, the "Electric Brae" appears to go up, when in fact it goes down.

The Auld Brig of Ayr was built about the middle of the thirteenth century. It was condemned at the beginning of the twentieth century, but Ayr Burns Club, along with Burns Clubs all over Scotland, raised enough money to repair it and it was reopened in 1910. In Burns' day, a New Brig was built, and in a poem Burns made the Auld Brig say to the New Brig, "I'll be a brig when ye're a shapeless cairn." This was prophetic, for 100 years later the New Brig was broken by a flood.

Want an ice lolly? You should alw... able to get one in Swansea, be... refrigerators are made here.

John Loudon Macadam, the inven... surfacing method known... in Ayr in 1756...

MY HOME TOWN

PLYMOUTH
PLYMOUTH

THIS WEEK'S WINNER—
PAT PARSONS (age 12), 10f PROSPECT ROW, DEVONPORT, PLYMOUTH, wins a £1 Postal Order.

Captain Robert Falcon Sc... explorer, was born... joined the Royal N... companions, he suc... Pole—only to find th... had beaten him by 35... the weather became s... men p...

Back in the days when new lands we... discovered, the people of Plymouth wer... the most adventurous of the explorer... wherever they settled, they remember... name of their home town. Today, there a... Plymouths scattered all over the world...

No. 1957, this sailing...

Although you'll find various exotic home town locations of past "Dandy" readers throughout this book, the majority of the features were concerned with readers' home towns in the United Kingdom. We've squeezed several on to these pages — have you visited any of them?

No.3

MY HOME TOWN

DOUGLAS
DOUGLAS

Douglas is the headquarters of the Isle of Man Parliament. The island has had its own Parliament since Celtic times. When the Vikings conquered the island, they founded the Tynwald. Today this consists of two bodies, the Legislative Council and the House of Keys, the latter, which corresponds to the House of Commons, is believed to be one of the oldest surviving governing assemblies in the world.

THIS WEEK'S WINNER—
PHILIP KNEEN (age 11), 50 SCHOOL ROAD, ONCHAN, ISLE OF MAN, wins £1 Postal Order.

MY HOME TOWN

Swansea
Swansea

THIS WEEK'S WINNER—
HAYDN WILLIAMS (age 11), 1 UPTON TERRACE, ST THOMAS, SWANSEA, wins a pair of Roller Skates.

Swansea is the home town of many famous sportsmen.

As far as the boys and girls of Swansea are concerned, the most important factory in their home town is a big toy factory which turns out metal playthings of all shapes and sizes.

...the Isle of Man owes its ...giant. He is said to have fought ...he title of the world's strongest ...he contest, jumped into the sea ...England. The Irish giant then ...s of rock and clay and heaved it ...The missile missed and landed in ...became the Isle of Man, while the ...Ireland became Lough Neagh.

...years a story has persisted that any ...could, by law, be shot on sight on the Isle ...Although this is not really true, the story is ...times when Scots were not welcome on the ...An old law states "That all Scots entering the Man do so at their peril, and must leave the ...by the next boat that goeth to Scotland, on ...f the forfeiture of their goods and their bodies ...son". In spite of this, the Scots Dukes of Atholl Kings of Manxland for many years, until they sold their rights to the British Government.

Of all the sporting events held in the Isle of... International Tourist Trophy Motor-Cycle... the best known. Starting from Douglas, the... is 37½ miles long, and has every imagina... corner, as well as stretches of road where cycles reach 140 m.p.h.

There are several interesting form... of transport on the Isle of Ma...

...khouse, ...opening ...ho has ...England ...ches.

Cliff Jones, the Welsh international footballer, who was transferred from Swansea Town to Tottenham Hotspur for £35,000.

Brian Curvis, the British and Empire welter-weight champion, who is to fight for the world title later this year.

Swansea has been called the "Metal capital of the world". It has iron, zinc, copper and tin-plate works, and most important of all is the last-named, for Swansea is the centre of the tin-plate industry. Nearly all the country's tin cans are made from Swansea tin-plate.

Douglas is the centre of one of the first electric railways in the world. The system was built 80... ...and its elderly vehicles still function...

On the promenade at Douglas there is... tram, or "Toast-rack" as it is somet... horses are trained to stop at a w... conductor. But for a time this signa... upset by a parrot on the route, wh... whistle and stopped the trams in...

Does any famous person live... ...make wooden legs in...

This selection of pictures is taken from The Dandy of the late 1930s. Drawn by Dudley Watkins, each was the heading picture to a text story of Wild Young Dirky, a young Scots lad in the time of Bonnie Prince Charlie, defending his country against the invading Redcoats.

1938

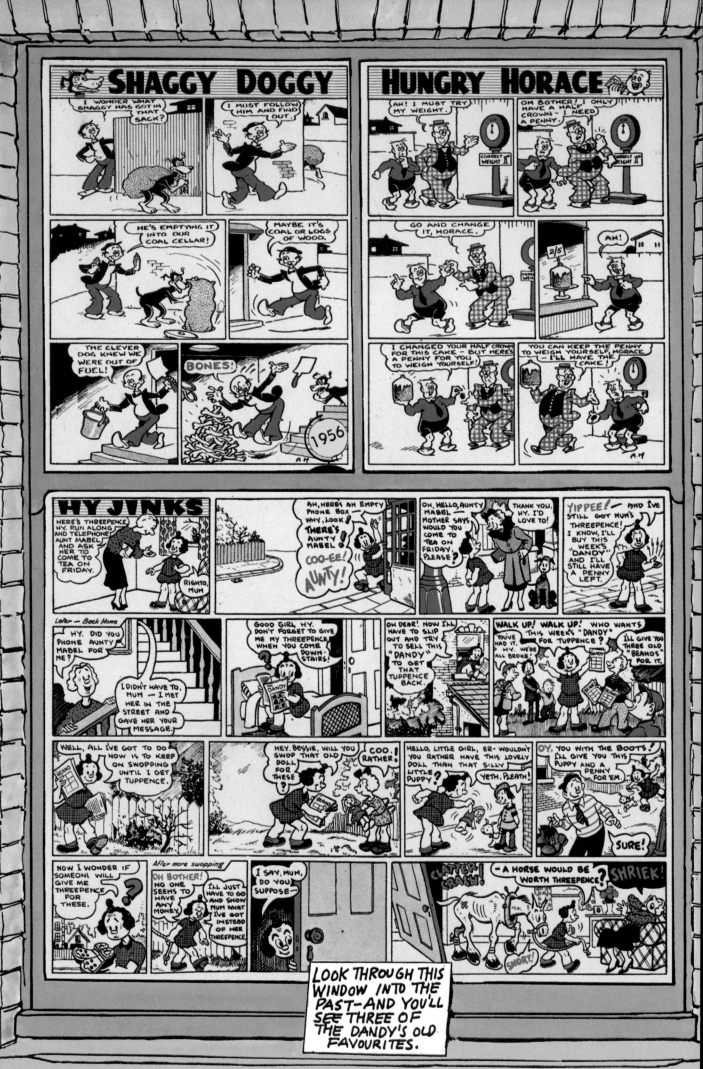

Korky the Cat doesn't need to go out of the U.K. to find foreign trouble — it follows him around, as these pages show!

England. France. 1988

Billy Whizz swiftly became one of the readers' favourite Beano pages where he's stuck FAST since May, 1964. France-y that!

BILLY WHIZZ!

I JUST LOVE...

TO THE BEACH

...TO DIG IN THE SAND! HEH-HEH!

FLUMP!

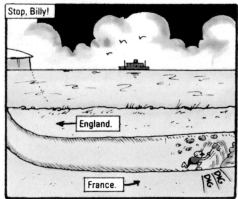

Stop, Billy!

England. France.

On a beach in France—

FLUMP! FLUMP! LE YIKES! TUM...TEE... TUM... LE EEK!

OO...ER... BON JOUR! LE SNARL!

COME HERE! HUH! NOT A VERY WARM WELCOME!

CRUNCH LE GRRR! CRUMP! OOPS! HOI!

HMM! I THINK I'D BETTER HEAD FOR HOME!

ER...'BYEE FOR NOW!

Back in England— TOOTLE! TOOT! PARP! WELL DONE, BILLY! WE THANK YOU! YOU'VE KNOCKED YEARS OFF OUR DATE TO FINISH THE TUNNEL TO FRANCE! EH? WHAT FOR?

SITE OF CHANNEL TUNNEL TO BE FINISHED 1993 CHORTLE!

so they made a "concerted" effort to earn some cash —
and look where they ended up!

MY HOME TOWN ST. HELIER *JERSEY*

ALDERNEY
GUERNSEY · SARK
JERSEY · ST. HELIER
CHERBOURG
FRANCE

No.4

ST HELIER is the capital of the Island of Jersey, the most southerly of the Channel Islands. Although much nearer France than England, the Channel Islands have been British for over 800 years. St Helier, and indeed, the whole of Jersey, is an extremely popular holiday resort; and St Helier airport is the second busiest in the British Isles.

It is from the rich farming countryside around St Helier that Jersey cattle originate. These cattle are fairly small and are normally fawn or cream in colour. They are renowned for the richness of their milk.

The Battle of Flowers takes place in St Helier every summer and it is a great tourist attraction. Beautiful floats parade through the streets, each one dressed up in a fantastic design made completely out of flowers and flower petals.

The actress Lillie Langtry was born in St Helier in 1852, and for many years was famous as a star of the stage and the silent screen. She was known as "The Jersey Lily".

CHEAP! WATCHES 10/- TO £3·10/-

If you go to St Helier, you may be surprised by the prices in the shops. Things like watches, cameras, leather goods, records, cigarettes and wines are much cheaper than in the rest of Britain!

PARBLEU! WE 'AVE BEEN BEATEN AGAIN!

Throughout the centuries that the Channel Islands have been British, France made repeated attempts to capture them. The last attempt was in 1781, when the invaders were defeated at the Battle of Jersey, fought in the market square of St Helier.

Write about your home town and win a DANDY prize. Anything interesting or out of the ordinary —that's what to write about. And just two or three items are enough.

Remember to put your name, age and address on your entry and say which prize you would like best from this list.

COMPLETE COWBOY OUTFIT, NURSE'S OUTFIT, BALL-BEARING ROLLER SKATES, £1 POSTAL ORDER.

1967

Jersey is ruled by its own government, known as the Assemblies of the States. The Lieutenant Governor and Commander-in-Chief of Jersey is the personal representative of the Crown in the island's government. The present Lieutenant Governor is Vice-Admiral Sir Michael Villiers, K.C.B., O.B.E. The first Lieutenant Governor of Jersey was Sir Francis Drake.

The Kids' next drop-off point in their world tour is Germany. Let's hope their gargoyle heads don't drop off this German Castle on to Addie and Hermy!

Addie & Hermy

You'd think that The Dandy's Addie and Hermy strips, being set in Germany during the Second World War, would never be set out of Europe — but you'd be wrong! Here are some examples of Addie and Hermy "invading" other countries to give Dandy readers a good old chuckle!

1941

There can't be many people in Britain who have received a letter from Adolf Hitler, in war-time Germany, but in the Beano issue dated 8th February 1941 that's exactly what happened to **LORD SNOOTY!** (No one else would have dared to call him a "dingswizzled twerp"!)

PETER The PENGUIN

1948

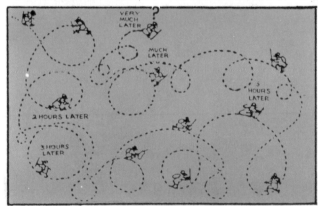

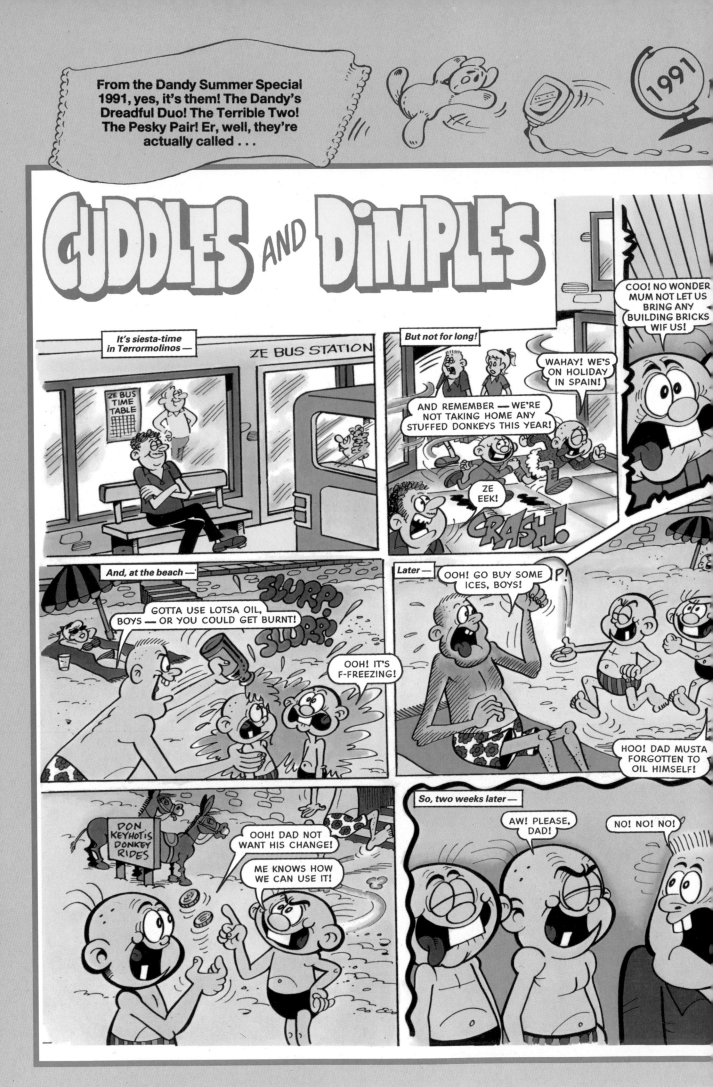

On holiday, but still in football gear, Ball Boy gives the waiter a SPAINful lesson in tackling!

BALL BOY

HERE I AM IN SUNNY SPAIN, READERS!

DE SOL

HOTEL DE SOL

THERE'S FERNANDO, OUR HOTEL WAITER. I WONDER IF HE'D PLAY FOOTBALL WITH ME SO I COULD SAMPLE SOCCER, SPANISH STYLE?

SURE, I PLAY FOOTBALL WITH YOU—ON THE BEACH AFTER LUNCH, OK?

YOU BET!

So —

AH, YOU HAVE THE BALL—WE START NOW.

WOW! YOU'RE GOOD!

NOW YOU TRY TO TAKE THE BALL OFF ME, OK?

SPANISH FOR "AARGH!"

CARAMBARGH!

TACKLE   CRUNCH!

GROAN!

LIMP LIMP

OOPS! MAYBE I SHOULD HAVE TAKEN MY BOOTS OFF AS WELL AS MY SHIRT!

Later —

FERNANDO'S FOOT IS TOO PAINFUL FOR HIM TO WAIT ON THE TABLES—SO, LITTLE SENOR . . .

HOTEL MANAGER

Tea-time —

WHERE'S OUR SON GOT TO?

AND OUR WAITER?

LUNCH IS SERVED, SIR AND MADAM!

THROW-IN STYLE

Just then —

HEH! THE MANAGER WAS SO PLEASED WITH ME FOR HELPING OUT, HE TOOK ME TO SEE REAL MADRID F.C. —I GOT ALL THE PLAYERS' AUTOGRAPHS!

Here are some of the Real Madrid players.—

MY HOME TOWN GIBRALTAR

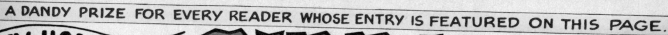

No.5

GIBRALTAR is a rocky peninsula in the Mediterranean, connected to the Spanish mainland by a narrow strip of land upon which is built the Colony's airport. The Rock of Gibraltar is probably the best-known landmark in the world, since any ship entering the Mediterranean must pass in sight of it.

The ownership of Gibraltar has been a subject of dispute for centuries and it was the scene of many bitter battles between the Moors and the Spanish, both of whom claimed it as their own. It was captured from Spain by the British in 1704, during the War of the Spanish Succession. By the Treaty of Utrecht in 1713, Spain formally recognised Britain's sovereignty over Gibraltar. It has been a British Colony ever since.

The most famous inhabitants of Gibraltar are the Barbary apes, which live and roam free on the Rock, the only wild apes in Europe. An old legend states that if the apes ever leave Gibraltar, so too will the British. So seriously is this legend taken that the apes are officially listed on the garrison strength of Gibraltar, and daily rations of food are issued to them!

The Rock of Gibraltar is honeycombed with man-made tunnels, many of which lead to huge storage caverns or gun ports. Some of these gun ports contain cannon used in battles of previous centuries, and they attract many tourists. Another attraction is the eastern face of the Rock, where large areas have been covered over with asbestos sheets. Rain falling here is channelled into underground tanks, which provide the Colony with all the fresh water it ever requires.

Gibraltar is often referred to as one of the "Pillars of Hercules". The other Pillar is Mount Hacho, across the Straits in Morocco. An ancient Greek myth tells how the two were joined together until Hercules, on his way to fight a huge three-bodied giant at Cadiz, tore them violently apart.

Tony Macedo, the goalkeeper who plays for Fulham Football Club, was born in Gibraltar. Tony has made several appearances for England.

Joseph Cuby, the young actor whose performance in the film, "Conspiracy of Hearts", was highly praised, was brought up in Gibraltar. He was only fifteen when he made the film.

During the Second World War, merchant ships and warships in Gibraltar were an attractive target to the enemy. In 1940 and 1941, the Italians made several "Human Torpedo" attacks on the harbour, but only with small success. The Royal Navy captured some of these machines, which had a powerful explosive warhead. Later in the war, British models were developed and used to great effect against enemy ships in harbour.

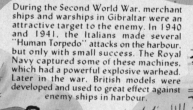

St Michael's Cave, in the Rock, is one of Gibraltar's most popular tourist attractions. The huge cavern is a natural amphitheatre, and concerts and dances are often held in it!

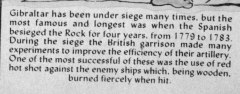

Gibraltar has been under siege many times, but the most famous and longest was when the Spanish besieged the Rock for four years, from 1779 to 1783. During the siege the British garrison made many experiments to improve the efficiency of their artillery. One of the most successful of these was the use of red hot shot against the enemy ships which, being wooden, burned fiercely when hit.

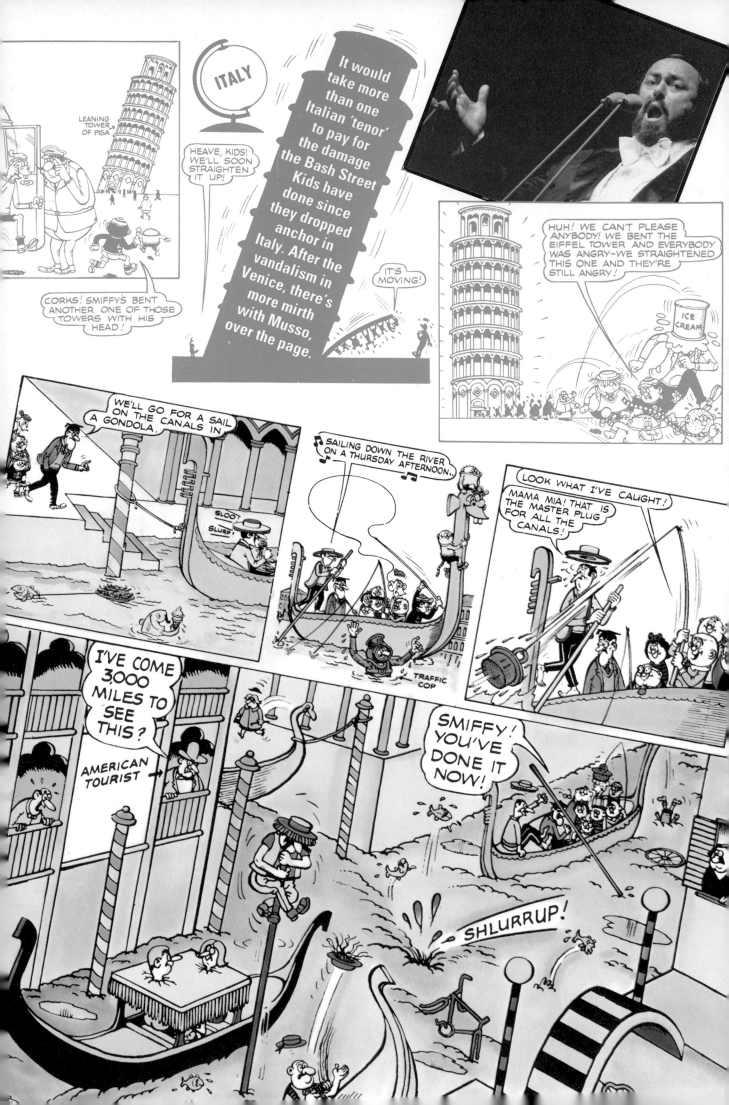

NEW STORY INSIDE

THE BEANO COMIC

Nº 209   JULY 3RD 1943

1943

Big Eggo

With the success of The Dandy's Addie and Hermy poking fun at wartime national leaders, in the early '40s The Beano followed up with their contribution to wartime whimsy — MUSSO, a big-headed, useless, arrogant know-all. And that was him at his best! Here he is with bombs, a balcony, Britishers and balloons!

Only Billy Whizz could take a day trip — to Venice! But how did he end up in New York?

Back in 1961, Ali Ha-Ha appeared on the back page of The Dandy every week. Ali's Dad happened to be Chief of Police in Baghdad, and unfortunately Ali bagged Dad every week — this time with umpteen rolling rubbish bins!

THE JOCKS

PHEW! WHAT A HEAT!

IT'S TOO HOT EVEN FOR BASHING THE JOCKS TODAY.

HEROES OF THE FOREIGN LEGION
NOW SHOWING

CHARGE!

OO! IT'S THE GEORDIES—WITH SHARP BAYONETS! YAHOO!

The Dandy's battling boys, The Jocks and The Geordies, let their imagination take them to the North African desert, as Geordie Legionnaires up against those fearsome foes, the Jock Arabs, and kick up a sand-storm of laughs!

1982

WHAT DOES THAT NOTICE SAY? IT'S VERY SMALL PRINT, ISN'T IT?

One thumping later—

OOH!

THAT HURT!

SMASHING! ANOTHER VICTORY FOR THE FOREIGN LEGION.

FOREIGN LEGION, EH? WE'LL HAVE TO TEACH THOSE GEORDIES A LESSON.

AYE!

Soon—

THERE THEY ARE!

GET READY TO SWITCH ON THE AIR-BLASTER, SIDNEY, WHEN I GIVE THE WORD.

THE JOCKS ARE HIDING BEHIND THAT SAND DUNE!

PING! PING!

DUCK, JOCKS!

FIRE AWAY, LADS! WE'LL MAKE THEM SURRENDER!

AND THE GEORDIES

LOOK! THE FOREIGN LEGION COULD FIGHT IN THE HEAT. LET'S TAKE A FEW TIPS FROM THEM.

Soon—

I'VE NEARLY GOT MY FOREIGN LEGION HAT MADE.

I'M MAKING A BAYONET.

HO-HO! WE'LL BE READY FOR THOSE JOCK ARABS.

JINGS! IT'S HOT! HERE COME THE JOCK ARABS. WE'LL CHASE THEM BACK TO THEIR TENTS. **HAW-HAW!**

OOH! OOH! I FEEL LIKE A PIN-CUSHION!

HURRAH! FOR THE FOREIGN LEGION!

NOW WE'LL PLAY A MAGIC CARPET TRICK ON THE JOCKS.

RIGHT, LADS! PULL! **HO-HO!** THEY DIDN'T SEE THE CARPET HIDDEN UNDER THE SAND.

YAAGH!

COME ON, LADS! GIVE THEM ANOTHER PASTING.

WHAT HAPPENED?

MOAN!

CHARGE!

NOW!

AARGH! A SAND STORM!

WHOOSH!

I CAN'T SEE WHERE I'M GOING.

RETREAT, JOCKS!

AFTER THEM!

EEK! IT WASN'T A SAND DUNE!

HO-HO! IT WAS GOOD OF THE SEASIDE MENAGERIE MAN TO LEND US THAT CAMEL. I HOPE THE GEORDIES HAVE PLENTY BREATH. THAT BEAST CAN RUN FOR TWENTY MILES WITHOUT STOPPING!

C-C-CAMEL!

HELP!

YOW! I DON'T LIKE THE LOOK OF THOSE SHARP TEETH!

RUN FOR YOUR LIVES!

ZANZIBAR

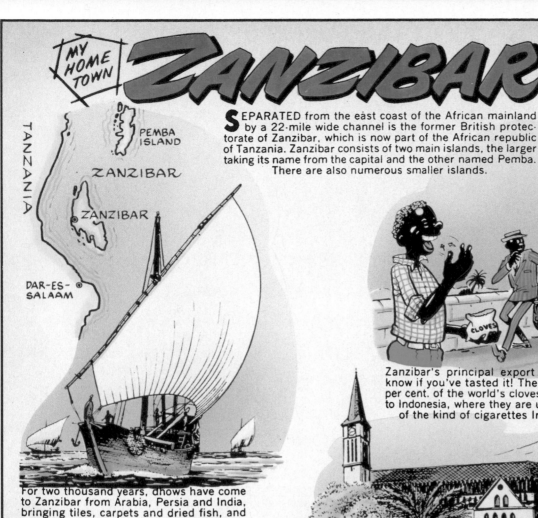

SEPARATED from the east coast of the African mainland by a 22-mile wide channel is the former British protectorate of Zanzibar, which is now part of the African republic of Tanzania. Zanzibar consists of two main islands, the larger taking its name from the capital and the other named Pemba. There are also numerous smaller islands.

Zanzibar's principal export is hot stuff—as you'll know if you've tasted it! The islands produce eighty per cent. of the world's cloves. Many tons of them go to Indonesia, where they are used in the manufacture of the kind of cigarettes Indonesians like best.

For two thousand years, dhows have come to Zanzibar from Arabia, Persia and India, bringing tiles, carpets and dried fish, and taking back cloves and mangrove poles.

If you like carnivals, you may have won a prize by knocking down one of Zanzibar's important exports, for the country sells a great deal of the produce of its vast coconut plantations overseas.

In the days of the slave trade, Zanzibar was one of the busiest slave-trading centres in Africa. After the abolition of this evil practice, this building, the U.M.C.A. Cathedral, was built on the site of the main slave-trading market.

1968

The rickshaw is still one of the quickest and most comfortable means of transport in Zanzibar, and it is certainly the most popular with tourists who visit the island!

This handsome building is a relic of Portuguese rule in Zanzibar. It is known to the inhabitants as the "House of Wonders"—Beit-el-Ajaib—because it has an old lift that crackles blue sparks!

Write about your home town and win a DANDY prize. Anything interesting or out of the ordinary —that's what to write about. And just two or three items are enough.

Remember to put your name, age and address on your entry and say which prize you would like best from this list.

COMPLETE COWBOY OUTFIT, NURSE'S OUTFIT, BALL-BEARING ROLLER SKATES, £1 POSTAL ORDER.

SEND YOUR ENTRY TO—
"MY HOME TOWN"
"The Dandy"
18a Hollingsworth St.,
London N. 7.

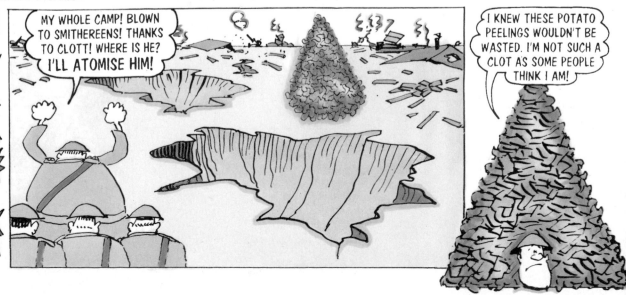

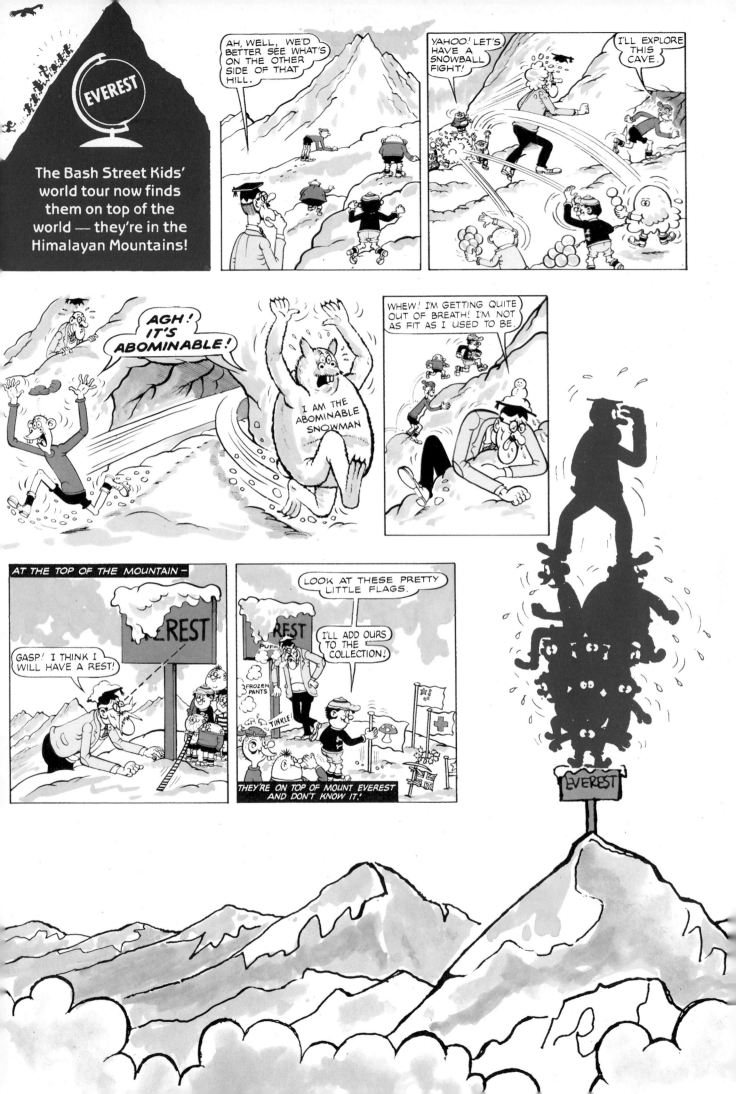

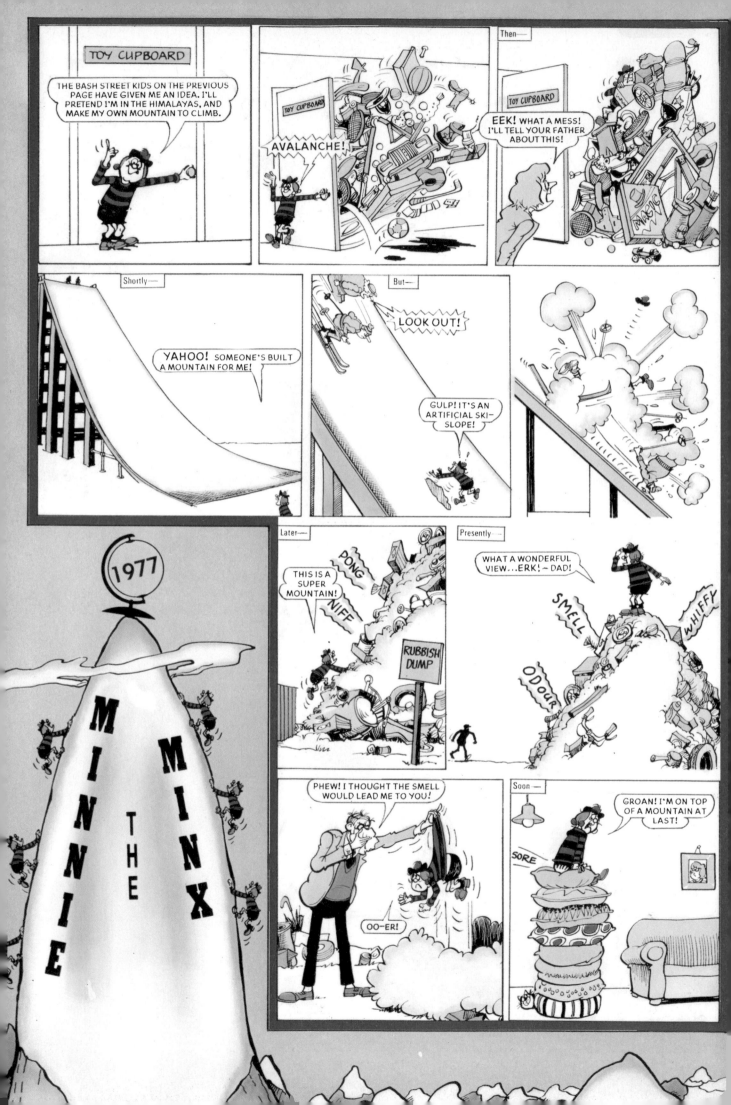

Malaysia's Prime Minister, Tunku Abdul Rahman, studied at one time in the Penang Free School, which is situated not far from Nibong Tebal.

This peculiar, short-trunked little animal is called a Malayan Tapir. These creatures inhabit the jungles of Malaya, sleeping all day and coming out at night to feast on grass and leaves.

Rubber is the most important product not only of Penang, but of the whole of Malaysia. Here an Indian rubber tapper collects the sticky sap known as latex from a tree on the plantation. Latex is the stuff that becomes rubber.

NIBONG TEBAL stands on the Krian River, in the island province of Penang, which is part of Malaysia. Nibong Tebal lies at the heart of large rubber plantations twenty miles south-east of George Town, the chief city of Penang.

The population of Penang is largely Chinese and in February, as part of the Chinese New Year celebrations, this colourful Dragon Dance takes place.

As well as Chinese, many Indians and Pakistanis inhabit Penang, all remaining loyal to the faiths of their homeland. This is a Chinese temple at Ayer Itam, in Penang.

Does any famous person live in your town?
Do they make glass eyes in your town?
Is any kind of funny festival held in your town?

Write about your home town and win a DANDY prize. Anything interesting or out of the ordinary —that's what to write about. And just two or three items are enough.

The name Nibong Tebal is made up of two Malay words. Nibong is the name of a kind of berry supposed to have great healing powers. These berries grow in large quantities in this area; hence "tebal," meaning thick or dense.

A product of Malaysia which is shipped overseas from Penang is tin. This is a tin dredge, which scrapes gravel from the bed of a pool. Tin ore is separated from the gravel in huge washing trays.

Win it, drink from it, eat it. What is it? It's another product of Penang that's popular overseas—the coconut.

Remember to put your name, age and address on your entry and say which prize you would like best from this list.

COMPLETE COWBOY OUTFIT, NURSE'S OUTFIT, BALL-BEARING ROLLER SKATES, £1 POSTAL ORDER.

1970

SEND YOUR ENTRY TO—
"MY HOME TOWN"
"The Dandy"
18a Hollingsworth St.,
London N.7.

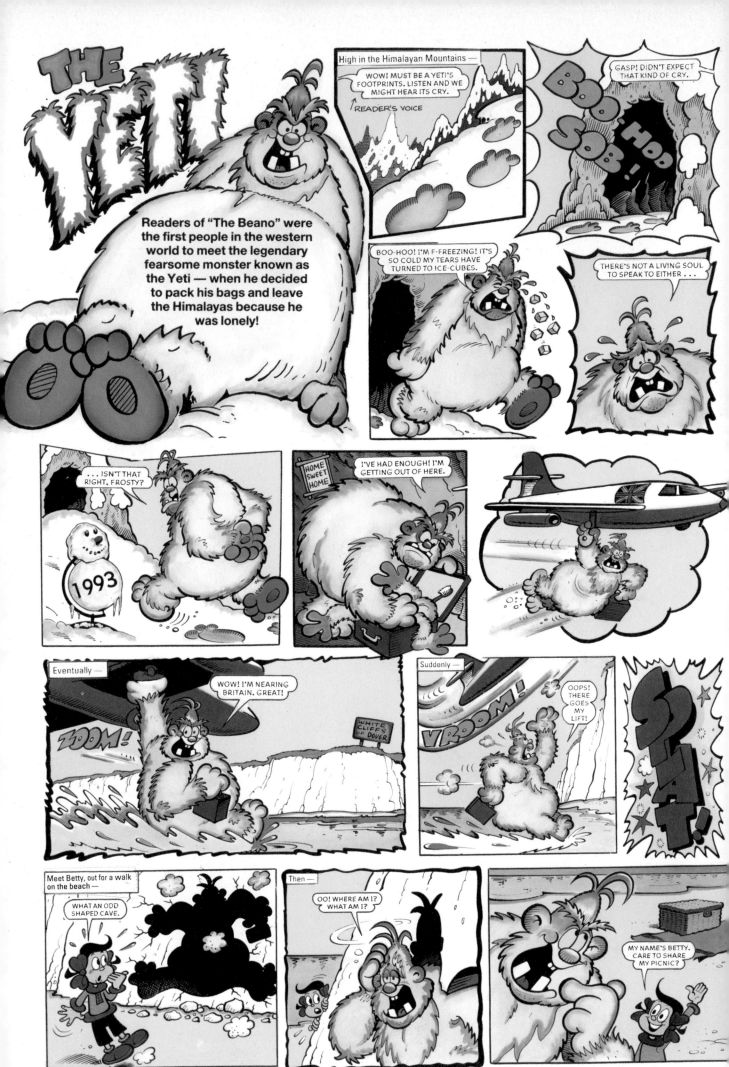

SHOCKER JOCK

WHO said, "You can't do two things at once if you're to do them properly."? Here's proof that you can! On an island in the River Dean this strangely-dressed youngster was having a good shot at doing two very different things at once. Of course, the lad is no ordinary 1954 schoolboy. He is Shocker Jock, who came back in time three hundred years from 2250, and he has his wonder gadgets from the future to help him. Jock was using an electric tension cutter to slice a tree trunk into planks — and, amazingly, he was "reading" a book at the same time.

2—True, the book was behind Jock, perched on a thing like a mu... stand. But he had a strange metal cylinder connected to the stand and his helmet, and it contained an instrument with wonderful powers. transformed the printed words on the page into spoken words on radio built into Jock's helmet! The boy was enjoying every word of thriller story when his nose detected a strong burning smell. Jc wheeled round and saw a patch of bushes blazing away. At once aimed his atomiser gun at the ground in front of the bushes.

3—Swis-s-sh! The atomic jet from the gun kicked up the soil and raised a miniature sand storm that completely smothered the blaze all in a moment. "I wonder how that started?" muttered Jock, turning back to his work. But the one person who could have answered the query stayed silent. He was Jonah Slugg, a burglar, and he had fired the bushes to distract Shocker Jock while he himself sneaked into the lad's hut. When Jock came in for his tea of vitamin pills, he found the place ransacked.

4—Several of Jock's amazing gadgets had been pinched, but the th... had made one grave error. In a corner he had left untouched egg-shaped metal object on caterpillar tracks. It was a 2250 inventi... called "The Sniffer", a marvellous mechanical bloodhound. Fitted w radar, as well as a trunk-like scent detector, this tin tracker could foll any trail. Jock set it to trail the unknown burglar. Soon he was speed across the river, his jet boat guided by the Sniffer's telescopic tail.

5—The Sniffer had a built-in control box which did the work of a clever brain, and when Jock's boat reached the river bank the metal hound switched off the engine. Then, without hesitation, the Sniffer trundled off towards Blackdean, its trunk weaving in the air. On the outskirts of the town, Jock found proof that he was on the thief's trail. Two policemen were holding back the crowd as masonry tumbled from a shattered building.

6—"I saw it all," Jock heard one of the onlookers say. tough-looking bloke fired a queer gun at the house, and next moment corner of the wall fell down. The man tried to get inside, but the fall bricks stopped him, and he ran off." Jock snorted. So the crook ho... to use the stolen gadgets to commit robberies! A stop must be pu... that. But first he would make safe the smashed building before any m of it collapsed.

1954

7—This was quickly done, thanks to a gun that could shoot round corners! Jock used it to fire three strands of super-strong 2250 string right round the block, and these thin threads supported the sagging walls as securely as bands of steel. But because it was one of his gadgets which had smashed the wall, Jock determined that another would help to repair the damage. From his hut he fetched a wonder machine, a machine that sucked up the crumbled rubble and turned it back into solid new bricks.

8—When he had made enough bricks to fill the gap and satisfy the amazed bricklayers, Jock set out once more in search of the burglar. Far across town ranged the trail, until at last Jock and the Sniffer reached Jonah Slugg's house. There the metal bloodhound speeded up, as if it knew the end was near. The house door was shut — so the Sniffer charged straight up the house wall towards an open window! The crook heard the scrape of the caterpillar tracks on the stonework, and got the shock of his life.

9—Slugg gave a moan of fear. Others of his gang had suffered at the hands of Shocker Jock and his gadgets, and the burglar dreaded to think what this fearsome-looking machine crawling up the wall might do to him. In desperation he scrambled out on to the window-sill — and leaped on to the top of a passing bus!

10—The bus swept out of sight round a corner, and Jock knew there was nothing for it but to start the hunt afresh. This time the questing Sniffer led him eventually to a cinema a mile away. Inside, Jonah Slugg thought he was safe in the dark among the crowd. Then the metal monster came trundling down the passage!

11—The people in the audience stared as Jonah gave a yell of fear and sprinted for an exit. But they got an even bigger shock when Jock and his mechanical bloodhound went tearing down the passage after the crook. Out of the cinema, clear of the town, the chase went on — until Slugg reached the River Dean.

12—Jonah whipped out a stolen 2250 gun and picked up a rock with his free hand. But suddenly the Sniffer's hose-like snout pointed up and sent a jet of water into his eyes! The crook gave a gasp of surprise and dropped the gun. Then he dived headlong into the river to evade this metal manhunter. Jock just laughed. He knew that the Sniffer was better than any spaniel when it came to retrieving from water — as the crook found out!

13—Jonah didn't like the look of that telescopic tail outstretched in a loop as the Sniffer churned towards him — and less did he like the feel of it round his bull neck five minutes later. For that was all the time the Sniffer needed to lasso the burglar and drag him back to the river bank. So scared was the gurgling, half-choked crook that he even welcomed the sight of two bobbies coming from Blackdean to tuck him away in a nice safe jail!

BRASSNECK

CHUCKLER CHARLEY BRAND had come to spend a few days with his uncle, Farmer Ben Brand. Young Charley had no worries about carrying his luggage. His marvellous metal pal, Brassneck, did the portering.

HULLO, UNCLE BEN! HOW ARE THINGS DOWN ON THE FARM?

HULLO, LADS! EVERYTHING IS FINE!

The chums had just arrived when two potato merchants, Spud Harrower and Pinky Kerr, came along. They made Uncle Ben an offer.

WHAT ABOUT LETTING US GROW POTATOES IN THAT FIELD AT THE FRONT OF THE FARM?

NOTHING DOING! I'M PLANTING POTATOES THERE MYSELF!

Spud and Pinky were annoyed at Uncle Ben's refusal and, as they drove back along the farm road, they planned to do something about it.

WE WANT THAT FIELD AND WE'RE GOING TO HAVE IT! HOW ABOUT PINCHING HIS PLOUGH, SPUD?

A GOOD IDEA, PINKY!

The roguish merchants needed all their strength to heave the plough on to their pick-up truck.

GOSH! THIS THING IS MUCH HEAVIER THAN IT LOOKS!

Later when Farmer Brand came looking for his plough, it was nowhere to be found.

THIS IS HOPELESS! I CAN'T GET STARTED TO PLOUGH THIS FIELD!

MAYBE BRASSNECK CAN HELP!

Brassneck certainly could help. The metal marvel hung on to the back of the tractor and was pulled along. He made three very neat furrows, one with each foot and one with his chin.

I SAY! KEEP THAT UP! YOU'RE MAKING A SMASHING JOB!

When Spud and Pinky saw that the field had been ploughed, they were amazed.

STONE THE CROWS! HOW DID THEY MANAGE TO DO THE PLOUGHING WITHOUT A PLOUGH?

Their cunning brains worked overtime as they set about thinking up another plan.

WE'LL STOP THE POTATO PLANTERS REACHING BRAND'S FARM!

WOW!

PRIVATE

SUCCESS!

BANG! BANG! Spud and Pinky watched gleefully as the bus's tyres were punctured.

BANG!

HURRY UP! HERE'S THE BUS NOW, PINKY!

HAW-HAW! NOTHING WILL GET PAST THESE TACKS!

The potato planters came by bus to the farm. Miles down the road, the plotters waited for it, then scattered handfuls of tacks in its path.

The bus driver knew it was hopeless. The potato planters were much nearer to their own homes than to the farm.

THERE'S NO POINT IN WAITING! YOU MIGHT AS WELL GO HOME!

1966

Farmer Brand grew anxious when the planters failed to appear.

THE POTATO PLANTERS SHOULD HAVE BEEN HERE TWO HOURS AGO!

Then Brassneck got busy on the potato-planting job. He rushed up and down the field, dribbling the seed potatoes from holes in the bottom of two sacks. Spud and Pinky watched astounded!

GREAT JUMPING CROWS! A ROBOT POTATO PLANTER!

Now that the potatoes had been planted in rows, the rogues' next desperate plan was to wreck the potato covering machine.

WELL, I RECKON NO-ONE WILL BE ABLE TO USE THIS MACHINE AGAIN!

Farmer Brand was at his wits' end when he discovered the damage.

SOMEONE'S WRECKED MY POTATO COVERING MACHINE! THE POTATOES MIGHT BE FROSTED IF THEY LIE IN THE OPEN ALL NIGHT!

But he need not have worried. Brassneck balanced himself in front of the tractor and covered up the potatoes as successfully as any machine could do the job.

KEEP IT UP, BRASSNECK! YOU'LL SOON HAVE THE FIELD FINISHED!

With Brassneck's help, all the work had been done in one day. Farmer Brand was bucked by it.

HOW'S THAT, UNCLE DAN?

WELL DONE, LADS! THAT'S THE NEATEST FIELD I'VE EVER SEEN!

I BET THEY'RE UP TO NO GOOD!

Brassneck had spotted Spud and Pinky. They went hurtling past on a tractor pulling a potato digger, still intent on ruining the potato field.

BETTER FOLLOW THEM!

Brassneck dashed off to fetch Farmer Brand's tractor.

LOOK OUT! ENEMY ON THE PORT BOW!

Brassneck had grabbed a big wooden rake and he now set the tractor hurtling at the rogues who were digging up the potatoes.

The scoundrels turned and went dodging and twisting through the farmyard.

THEY DON'T SEE ME BUT I SEE THEM!

But Brassneck got ahead at last and met them head on. CRUNCH! Like a knight in days of yore, the metal lad charged the villains and sent them reeling with a raking blow.

TAKE THAT!

YAHOO!

AARGH!

The police were sent for and the rogues arrested.

HURRAH! NOW MY POTATOES CAN GROW IN PEACE!

By the time they got out of jail, Farmer Brand's potatoes would be harvested, peeled and eaten!

Remember me, folks? I'm Johnny Grant, and that funny-looking guy in my book is Baggy Pants, who is an Eastern magician. He "magicked" himself down to a mere six inches and became a picture in my book to avoid trouble.

MY PAL,

1959

But this day I was feeling kinda browned off. I needed some fun in my life. So I said the magic word "Bagee" and brought old Baggy Pants to life again. "Greetings, O Master!" chirped my pet wizard as he stepped out of the page. Now things would hum.

And they did, too! For Snowy the cat leaped at Baggy and grabbed him. My magician was still only six inches tall, and somehow he couldn't make himself any bigger. Even his scimitar was as small as a pin.

IN the early series, Baggy Pants, the Eastern magician, was a tiny chap just six inches tall, but as you can see on the opposite page, in a later series he was ever-so-slightly larger, thanks to a magic spell.

Poor old Baggy Pants was treated like a mouse. Snowy had him in its teeth and raced away. I made a pounce but the cat was too nippy for me.

Baggy must have had visions of being chewed up. He drew his scimitar, but he couldn't get a clear swipe at Snowy. He could only wriggle and yell.

Luckily I caught up with them then. I grabbed Snowy, and when the cat opened its mouth to yowl it dropped its prize. In a twink, Baggy was ready for escape.

My wizard unfurled a tiny magic carpet and flew off on it, circling higher and higher round the room.

But Snowy was spitting and hissing and struggling in my arms. The cat broke free and leapt after its prey.

Baggy was in danger. He swerved up and away—and knocked into the lampshade. And the blinking thing crashed down on my head! As for Snowy, the cat went right through the window!

The noise brought Mum on the run. I was in for big trouble. But good old Baggy was on the job at once. "Hickory-dockery, broken crockery—Save Mrs Grant from dreadful shockery."

So Mum was relieved to see no damage done. I guess she was kinda puzzled by the queer-looking Eastern lampshade Baggy's magic had produced, but that didn't bother me.

"You got me out of a jam, Baggy." I told my pet magician as he stood on my hand. "We're going to have fun from now on, you and me." "You bettee, Master!" chirped my little pal, Baggy Pants.

BAGGY PANTS

"BISMILLAH!" croaked my pal Baggy Pants. That means, "Oh, dear me!" in Baggy's Eastern lingo, and it also meant he was worried. So was I. How was my giant magician to get into our little house? He hadn't thought about that when he magicked himself into a giant!

Still, Baggy is game to try anything. He squeezed through the door — and gave my Mum the scare of her life!

Then another difficulty cropped up. My pal was hungry, and he had an appetite like an elephant.

He ate 28 lb. of chips! I know because I fed them into his big mouth with a spade!

Now it was bed-time, and that brought another problem, for we had no giant-size beds. However, I saw a way out, and got busy with a hack-saw.

Having sawn off the bed-end to make room for Baggy to stretch out. I then drew up the sofa to support the bits of him that wouldn't be resting on the bed.

Still it wasn't enough. So finally my pal went to sleep with his big tootsies sticking out of the window.

Came the dawn — and an early bird! This dicky-bird did its morning singing perched on Baggy's toes. And the next-door cat was on the hunt.

The pussy sprang, and just in time the birdie flew. But the cat's claws dug into Baggy's toes, and my poor magician awoke with a yell.

To make things worse, Baggy jerked his foot up, and his outsize toes shattered the window-frame. He felt very sore, and so did Mum, for he had also broken a chair and bust the sofa.

We had to get a bigger bed for Baggy. But not one of the stores had one half big enough to fit him. Then a great idea struck me.

That night I turned burglar. It was easy to break into this place with a giant wizard to help me.

FURNITURE SHOWROOM

MUSEUM

THE GIANT'S BED

The problem of a bed for Baggy Pants was solved at last. He slept in the Giant's Bed in the Museum, and he slept like a top — the biggest top in the world!

1990 NUMBER 13

The Beano's 'Number 13' was full of monsters — and monster laughs!

IT COULD BE YOU!

Yes, if you were to sample Mickey's Magic Lollipops, any of these pictures might be you! This weird and wonderful story took some licking! It was a suck-cess in the Beano for nearly ten years!

TIN CAN TOMMY

THE CLOCKWORK BOY
(AND HIS BROTHER, BABE)

Was the world ready for this? Two CLOCKWORK brothers meet two CONCRETE brothers! Hard to believe, eh — but this was the war-time Beano!

As a perfect example of out-of-this-world comic silliness these two pictures from the Beano cover of September 6, 1952, must snake . . . er . . . take the biscuit! Only in the Beano could you have a trouser-wearing bear conversing with a false-nose-and-specs-wearing green snake!

What do you call it when the Bash Street Kids tumble into a paddy field and get soaking wet?

Answer:—
The Great Wail of China!

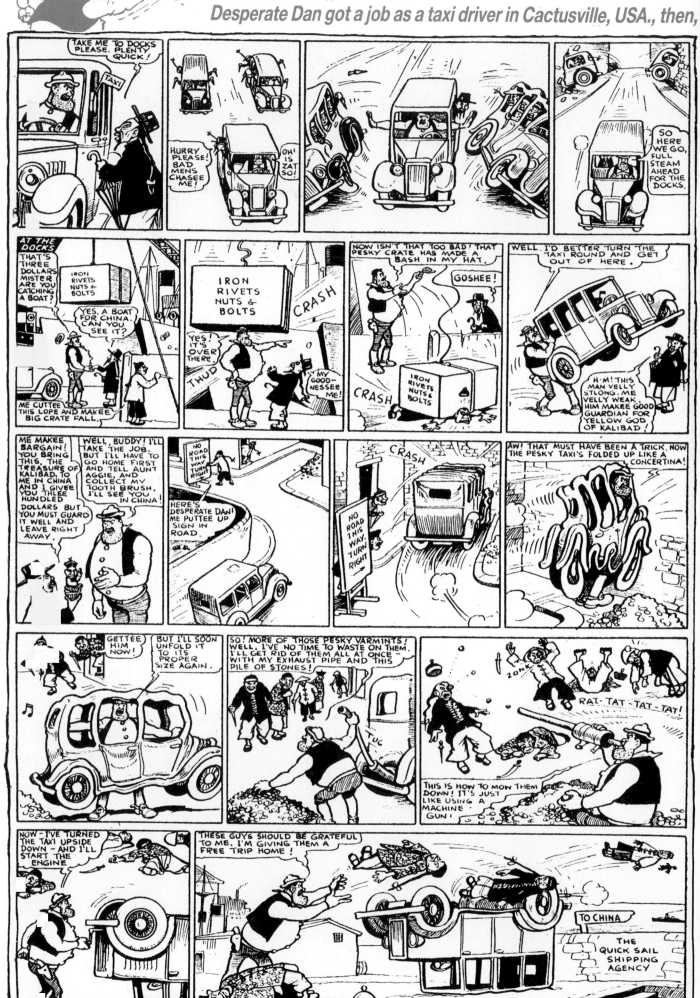

1949

In Chinatown the other day Ah Sing began a grand speedway. And as they'd not seen one before, the things they did would make you roar. The riders were quite set aback by seeing spectators on the track. In fact the Chinatown P.C. sat there all through and had his tea. You see the P.C. had been reading his rules, which said to stop any speeding. Go Slow on his old bike was first, the old chap pedalled fit to burst, but though the track beat all the rest, he went so slow he came off best. The motor cyclists were led a dance — the second prize went to the ambulance. Then after the show they all agreed — that they'd rather have a feed than speed.

REPAIRS WHILE YOU WAIT

ROAD UP

JUDGE

ICES

These cheery chaps,
A-biking they did go
In The Dandy
Fifty-three years ago!

The Cheery Chinamen all love a bike. They all feel tired
when they've to hike. So here's the reason for the shouting,
their cycling club's been on an outing. All sorts of
wheelers joined the queue. Al Flat's steam roller turned up,
too. Alas, alack, the silly chap turned the cycles into scrap.
Tu Tired's two-wheeler hit a bump and off the road it gave a
jump. He went to sleep upon a post and he enjoyed the
outing most. Sam Swift's new motor bike was there, but
poor Sam left it in mid-air. Alone it cleared the traffic jam
and went home — but minus Sam! The Chinamen had quite
a day, but what a price they had to pay. When they move
each muscle creaks and they won't sit for weeks and weeks!

JIMMY AND HIS MAGIC PATCH

1946

How would you like to be Champion Wrestler of Japan? Here's how ten-year-old Jimmy Watson accomplished it in The Dandy over fifty years ago, thanks to a certain Magic Patch on his trousers!

1. Seated at a bench in the Boys' Club in his home town was Jimmy Watson, the Boy with the Magic Patch. Jimmy was making an "Electric Shock Machine", a simple little gadget consisting of an electric battery and two coils of wire. He wore rubber gloves on his hands to protect himself from the powerful electric current in the machine. He grinned as he thought of the fun he would have with his pals, but little did he know of the "shocks" that were in store for him!

2. If Jimmy had looked behind him at that moment he would have seen two of his chums whispering together. Johnny Green and Bill Carter had just been practising ju-jitsu, a kind of wrestling invented by the Japanese. "I say," whispered Johnny, "what about showing Jimmy one of our ju-jitsu tricks?" Jimmy suspected nothing until Johnny's strong young arms grabbed him round the waist and the next moment he went whizzing through the air!

3. How the boys in the club laughed when Jimmy landed with a thud on his back on the hard floor. "Ho! Ho!" roared Johnny. "Don't you wish you could wrestle like that, Jimmy?" At the same time Bill Carter pointed to a ju-jitsu notice on the wall. "Why don't you join our ju-jitsu class, Jimmy? That will give you a chance to get your own back." Jimmy turned over on the floor and glared at the notice. "I'd like to get even with them," he muttered. "If only I were a ju-jitsu expert!"

4. The next thing Jimmy knew he and his shock machine were whirling through space. Without realising it he had made a wish, and once more the Magic Patch on his pants was granting it. When Jimmy came back to earth again he found he was in a quaint room where two yellow-skinned wrestlers were fighting. "Gosh!" muttered Jimmy. "They look like Japanese!" The Magic Patch had whisked Jimmy back to a ju-jitsu school in Japan where ju-jitsu was first taught.

5. Before Jimmy could move, a tall bearded Japanese Baron strode up to him and gripped his arm, "Who are you, boy? Are you a new pupil for my wrestling school?" Without waiting for an answer, the Baron beckoned to one of the wrestlers and snapped an order to him. The wrestler crouched, then circled round Jimmy. Suddenly he sprang at the boy and gripped his legs. For the second time that day Jimmy flew over a wrestler's shoulder and landed with a bump on the floor.

6. Jimmy saw dozens of stars as he lay on the floor gasping for breath. Then the mist cleared before his eyes and he saw the Baron bending over him. "Bah!" grunted the Baron. "The boy has a lot to learn." He called to Jimmy's opponent and pointed to a door. "Take him to the infants' class, Moto," he ordered. Jimmy just had time to gather up his shock machine before he was hustled into a nearby room where tiny Japanese babies were practising ju-jitsu.

7. "See how the young ones can wrestle, boy," said Moto with a sneer. "You had better join their class. Be careful or they may hurt you." Jimmy's face darkened with rage and he shook a fist at Moto and the Baron as they left the room. "Make a fool of me, would they?" he muttered. "I'll find some way to get my own back." And suddenly it dawned on Jimmy that the shock machine would help him to succeed.

8. The little Japanese babies stared in wonder as they saw Jimmy strip off his school blazer and place that strange-looking shock machine in one of his pockets. Then he threaded the two metal grips up inside the sleeves of the blazer, one coil through each sleeve. Jimmy then put on his blazer and made sure his gloves were pulled firmly over his hands. He was ready now. What was Jimmy's plan?

9. The Baron looked down his nose when Jimmy walked up to him. "I've done all my training now," said Jimmy with a sly grin. "I want to fight one of your best wrestlers. That big thug there," he added, pointing to the figure of a huge wrestler standing with arms folded. The Baron could not believe his ears. "Why, that is Yama, the Champion of Japan! If you fight him he will surely kill you!" Jimmy snorted. "Don't be too sure about that," he said.

10. "Very well, boy," said the Baron. "Let the contest begin." Yama bared his teeth in an evil snarl. "I'll kill the brat," he whispered as he made for Jimmy. But he didn't know about those two metal grips which Jimmy was holding in his gloved hands. Suddenly Yama darted at Jimmy and gripped his hands, meaning to throw the lad over his shoulder. Instead the champion gave a loud yell of pain and started to dance about in agony!

11. The giant wrestler's bare hands had touched the metal grips which Jimmy held, and the current gave him such a shock that he jumped high in the air. Jimmy just gave his opponent a little push and Yama lost his balance and fell, cracking his head on the hard floor of the school. Yama gave a grunt and lay quite still. Gasps of awe came from the onlookers. Here was a boy who had defeated the Champion wrestler of Japan!

12. What a fuss they made of Jimmy. They set him on a high pile of cushions and there he sat while the wrestling school kow-towed to the new Champion. "Boy, oh, boy!" chuckled Jimmy. "Wait till I tell Johnny Green about this." But suddenly the Magic Patch whisked him back again to the present day, and to this day Johnny Green still thinks Jimmy is pulling his leg when he says he was Champion wrestler of Japan for an hour!

Ball Boy didn't have to go halfway around the world to tackle his Oriental opponents in 1978 —

BALL BOY

HAVING A SCOTTISH HOLIDAY THIS YEAR, B.B?

READER'S VOICE

NO, NO, READERS — I CAN'T HELP THINKING ABOUT THE WORLD CUP, THIS YEAR   1978.

NEED A "WORLD CUP" TROPHY TO PLAY FOR!

THIS'LL HAVE TO DO!

Two o'clock—

NOW WE'LL SEE HOW GOOD THEY ARE!

GASP! ABSOLUTELY BRILLIANT!

GOAL!

OH, NO!

Full time—   WINNERS!

BAH! WE LOST ONE-NIL.

LAP OF HONOUR

COME TO OUR CELEBRATION BANQUET!

— They're all from the restaurant just down the street!

1978

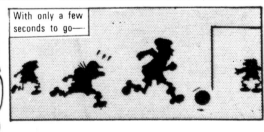

THE BOY WHO COULDN'T SKATE—*(Continued from page 71).*

the bank when round the bend of the canal came sweeping a mighty wave, six or seven feet high.

The gates must have broken as Hans was shouting warning. The tidal wave m̶o̶v̶e̶d̶ at lightning speed, and in a mom̶ spot where the happy, laughi̶ had been holding their ice under water.

Grin̶

and

ar̶

" Good old Hans ! Hans saved our lives ! " arose the cry, and he was carried in triumph to the village behind the br̶ d̶.

A week later h̶ tation h̶om

It was an exciting time for Black Bob, the champion sheepdog, and his master, Andrew Glenn. A special invitation was taking them right across the world to give a demonstration of sheep handling in Australia.

The next day the big shepherd put Black Bob through his pace before a huge crowd. Bob guided the sheep round th obstacles and into pens expertly, and delighted the crowd.

The following three pages show excerpts from a fourteen-page, weekly Black Bob story set mainly in the Australian outback, where Bob gains a new master!

BLACK BOB
THE DANDY WONDER DOG

It was a strange, high pitched whistle—and it had a startling effect on Black Bob. Paying no heed to Pat, he trotted obediently back.

Hey, Bob! Come back!" yelled Andrew Glenn. But he didn't. Bob ran straight to the native, mesmerised by the man's strange power.

The famous sheepdog had turned on his rightful master, Andrew Glenn, and held him helpless on the ground while Burra warned him, "Don't you dare follow us no more!"

1976

Burra seemed to have got clean away. But the tribesmen kept tame emus which they had learned to ride. The native leapt astride one and rode off in pursuit of the jeep.

The tiger snake bared its fangs to strike—but Black Bob struck first. The snake squirmed, but the fight was over in seconds.

All this time, Andrew Glenn, Black Bob's rightful master, and a native tribesman had been searching for Bob and Burra. But it was Bob who found them.

Guessing that something had happened, Andrew Glenn followed Black Bob to the spot where Burra had been left—and got a nasty shock. The hunter was on his feet behind a rock, aiming a rifle!

It was the sound of a shot. Burra looked back. A pack of savage dingoes was attacking a farmer's sheep!

Bob's rightful master, Andrew Glenn, was there helping the farmer to fight off the dingoes, when suddenly the leader of the pack sprang at him.

The dingo's fangs were flashing inches from Andrew Glenn's throat when out of the blue came a flying fury. It was Black Bob!

The two dogs had fought before, but this time it was to the finish! Over and over they rolled, till Bob got a death grip on the dingo's throat.

Now the dingo pack was no more. Andrew Glenn and Burra were both proud of the gallant dog which had helped to wipe it out.

Now that the death of his own dog had been avenged, Burra returned Black Bob to Andrew Glenn. The shepherd and the hunter parted friends, then Burra strode off into the bush—alone.

MY HOME TOWN PERTH *Western Australia*

PERTH is the capital of Western Australia, and is situated on the estuary of the Swan River, about twelve miles from the sea. Founded in 1829, and named after Perth in Scotland, the town only began to prosper and grow in the 1890's, when gold was discovered in Western Australia. Today it is the chief commercial centre of Western Australia.

PERTH

One of the greatest athletes of all time, Herb Elliot, comes from Perth. He smashed the world record for the mile several times and in the Olympic Games in Rome in 1960 he won a gold medal for the 1500 metres. He finished in the fantastic time of 3 minutes 35.6 seconds —a record so far unsurpassed. He has now retired from top-class athletics.

Rolf Harris, the famous TV entertainer, comes from Perth. Rolf, who shot to fame a few years ago with the record, "Tie me Kangaroo Down, Sport", is an artist and a qualified teacher. He also plays the wobbleboard and the digeridoo, the long wooden horn of the aborigines.

The Festival of Perth is held in the town every year in March. A feature of the festival is the dancing of the aborigines, the native tribesmen of Australia.

The Swan River, on which Perth stands, was visited in 1697 by a party of Dutch explorers. They were amazed to see there some very unusual birds — black swans. These birds are found only in Australia and the black swan is the emblem of Western Australia.

No.8

A popular sport with the citizens of Perth is surfing —riding the waves on a specially-made surf-board. This sport requires skill and balance — and, of course, a beach with the right kind of waves. There are plenty of these, however, near Perth.

Does any famous person live in your town?
Do they make glass eyes in your town?
Is any kind of funny festival held in your town?

Write about your home town and win a DANDY prize. Anything interesting or out of the ordinary —that's what to write about. And just two or three items are enough.

Remember to put your name, age and address on your entry and say which prize you would like best from this list.

COMPLETE COWBOY OUTFIT, NURSE'S OUTFIT, BALL-BEARING ROLLER SKATES, £1 POSTAL ORDER.

SEND YOUR ENTRY TO—
"MY HOME TOWN"
"The Dandy"
18a Hollingsworth St.,
London N. 7.

Another of Perth's favourite sports is Australian Rules Football. This game, played on an oval field 180 yards long by 120 yards wide, was developed in Australia before rugby was introduced to the country. The ball is larger than a rugby ball and a player may punch or kick it forward. He may not run with it, however, unless he bounces it every ten yards. Four posts of no set height are fixed at each end of the pitch. Any kick which goes between the two inner posts without touching an opponent scores six points. If it touches an opponent, however, or goes beween the outer posts, it only scores one point.

Perth is sometimes known as the City of Lights. When American astronaut John Glenn was orbiting the earth in 1962, the inhabitants of Perth switched on every light in the city to wish him well. From his space capsule, Glenn radioed to Earth a big "thank you" to the citizens. Other astronauts have also seen this dazzling electric show.

1967

Almost back to where they started from, the Bash Street Kids arrive in Hawaii —

WELCOME TO HAWAII!

THESE YAMS ARE DELICIOUS!

YAM! YAM!

LATER

THEY WALK ON RED-HOT COALS IN THEIR BARE FEET!

HOW INTERESTING!

HOI! KEEP YOUR BIG FEET AWAY FROM MY TOAST!

THESE HOT CHESTNUTS ARE DELICIOUS!

ANOTHER TEST OF BRAVERY —

HE WHO DIVES FROM THE HIGHEST POINT IS MADE CHIEF OF TRIBE!

HIGHEST POINT EVER DIVED FROM

I MUST HAVE A CLOSER LOOK AT THESE BRAVE MEN. I COULDN'T DIVE LIKE THAT - I'VE NO HEAD FOR —

—HEIGHTS!

S-SSLIPP

SPLOSH

HAIL TO THEE, O GREAT CHIEF!

ARISE, O GREAT WHITE CHIEF!

FLICK   SWEEP

THE LITTLE ONES CAN SERVE YOU, O 'MASTER!

HEH! HEH! THIS IS A GREAT LIFE! I THINK I'LL STAY HERE FOREVER!

THIS IS A TERRIBLE LIFE!

ICE PACK

I'VE NEVER WORKED SO HARD!

A MESSENGER HAS ARRIVED, O WISE ONE.

TCH! TCH! SEND HIM IN.

CLIP!

TELEGRAM FOR TEACHER! PHEW! I'M TIRED AFTER THAT LONG SWIM!

TELEGRAM?

HEMPH!

POST OFFICE INLAND TELEGRAM

TO TEACHER. RETURN TO BASH ST. SCHOOL AT ONCE. HEADMASTER.

I'LL IGNORE IT—I'VE DECIDED TO STAY HERE!

GRR! WE WERE BETTER OFF AT SCHOOL!

SPLUTTER! MUMBLE!

EY, O EDUCATED ONE! WE'VE GOT GUESTS!

AH! BEARING GIFTS, I HOPE.

BUT— OUR CHIEF CHALLENGES YOUR CHIEF TO A COMBAT WITH WAR CLUBS!

OUR CHIEF ACCEPTS!

BOOMF

SPLUTTER! ER-DON'T BE TOO HASTY, CHAPS!

LOOK OUT! HERE COMES SCREWY DRIVER

RING! THIS IS SCREWY'S WAY OF MAKING SURE HE WAKES EARLY THIS MORNING.

MY PATENT GETTER-UPPER WORKED ALL RIGHT. NOW I SHOULD GET DOWN TO THE *PAPER* SHOP IN RECORD TIME WITH MY ROCKET SKATES.

GANGWAY! I'M IN A HURRY.

HUH! I'M NOT THE FIRST, THERE'S A BLINKING QUEUE, BUT I EXPECTED THAT. I HOPE THE TRAP I SET LAST NIGHT WORKS ALL RIGHT.

HA! HA! IT DID! THAT'S GOT RID OF THE QUEUE.

NEWSAGENT

YAWN! IT'S TIME I OPENED THE SHOP I SUPPOSE.

I WANTED TO MAKE SURE I WAS FIRST, MR SMITH. IF I'D WAITED TOO LONG YOU MIGHT HAVE BEEN SOLD OUT.